First English edition for the United States, Canada, and the Philippines published by
Barron's Educational Series, Inc., 1997.

First published in Germany under the title *Barenstarke Weihnachten* ©1995
Verlag Heinrich Ellerman Munchen.
English translation ©1997 by Barron's Educational Series, Inc.

All inquiries should be addressed to:
Barron's Educational Series, Inc.
250 Wireless Boulevard
Hauppauge, New York 11788

International Standard Book No. 0-7641-5003-0

Library of Congress Catalog Card No. 97-70900

PRINTED IN HONG KONG
9 8 7 6 5 4 3 2 1

A Glimatron Christmas
Sharing the Holiday Spirit

Erhard Dietl

BARRON'S

Ding-ding-ding! "It's time!" Mother calls, ringing her little bell as a special signal. "You can come in and open presents now!"

Arthur smiles his biggest smile. Mother looks like an angel, he thinks. She's so excited, she almost seems to be flying!

What a great Christmas!
Mother gets some exercise
equipment. And look at
Father's gift—a neat little
gadget to help him fill
his pipe!

"Your turn, Arthur," Father says. "Open your gift now!"

Arthur rips his package open. Then he gasps. "I can't believe it!" he shouts. "A Glimatron 5000—just what I've always wanted!"

"Santa Claus was really good to you this year!" Mother beams.

"I can't wait to go outside and try it out!" Arthur says.

"Go ahead," says Mother. "But be back in a half hour, so we can sing Christmas carols. And don't forget to wear your scarf—it's freezing out there!"

"Don't use your Glimatron till you've read the instructions," Father reminds him.

"I already know how it works," Arthur answers. "I know all about the Glimatron 5000."

The Glimatron is just as cool as he thought it would be! The blades turn, and smoke puffs out. It rings, toots, and huffs. It rolls, shakes, and twinkles like a thousand stars. The hand on top even waves to Arthur!

Arthur makes his Glimatron do a handstand. Then he makes it run straight up a wall!

The Glimatron glides through the deepest snow on its runners.

Oops! It disappears down some dark stairs.

A bear is asleep at the bottom, curled up in the garbage-littered alley.

Ouch! The Glimatron crashes into his head and wakes him up. "What's that?" the bear growls.

"'Scuse me," says Arthur, feeling shy. He has never met a poor, homeless bear before. "May I have my Glimatron 5000 back?"

"Your *what*? What kind of contraption is that?" the bear grumbles.

Arthur can't believe his ears. "You've never heard of the Glimatron 5000?" he asks. "Look—it toots and moves. It rings and shakes. It twinkles like a thousand stars. It even flies!"

"Oh, yeah? Let's see it fly!" snorts the bear.

Arthur pushes some buttons, but the bear just
shakes his head. "You call that flying?" he asks.
"That looks more like hovering to me."

Arthur thinks fast. "At Christmas, it just hovers.
But—but the rest of the time, it flies!"

"Well," the bear admits, "it does look beautiful,
sparkling like that. It reminds me of a Christmas tree."

Arthur looks around the cold, bare alley. "Where's
your Christmas tree? Did you get lots of presents?"

The bear hangs his shaggy head. "Who would give
me presents? No one cares about me."

"Aren't you cold?" Arthur worries. "How do you live out here in the winter?"

"Don't worry about me," the bear mumbles. "I've got my sleeping bag. I'll be okay."

Then Arthur remembers the time. "Oh! I have to go now—Mother and Father want us all to sing Christmas carols together."

The bear's eyes get very sad. "Oh, Christmas tree, oh, Christmas tree . . ."

Arthur turns to go. But something makes him turn back. "Here, you can borrow my Glimatron."

The bear stares at him. "Really?" he asks.

"Just till tomorrow," Arthur explains. "Or maybe the day after. But be careful about the batteries—it uses them up awfully fast. Be sure to turn it off when you're not using it."

"I promise," says the happy bear. "Wait! I have something for you, too."

Rummaging in his sleeping bag, he pulls out a big red button. "Here," he says, holding it out to Arthur. "This is no ordinary button. This is a genuine magic button from the Orient."

"A magic button!" Arthur gasps. "Wow! How do you use it?"

"Just rub it," explains the bear, "and make a wish."

"Will my wish really come true?"

"Try it and see." The bear winks as he hands Arthur the button.

Arthur holds the red button
tightly as he walks back up
the stairs.

"There you are!" Mother exclaims, opening the door.

"Did you have fun with your Glimatron?" Father asks. "Hey, where is it?"

Arthur takes a deep breath. "I—I traded it . . . for this magic button."

"You did WHAT?" Mother cries.

"Are you out of your mind?" Father roars.

"It's okay," Arthur tries to explain. "I gave it to the old bear who lives in the alley. He didn't get any Christmas presents. And this button really is magic—he told me so."

"That's a bear-faced lie!" Father shouts. "I'll show him! He can't cheat little children like that and get away with it!"

Before Arthur can say another word, Father is
off to search for the bear.

"Oh, Arthur," Mother sighs. "Why did you have
to get into trouble today, of all days? Your
father gets so upset."

They sit in an unhappy silence. What will Father
do to the bear? Arthur worries. Then he gets an
idea. Taking the button from his pocket, he
begins to rub it. "I wish, I wish . . ." he whispers.
Will it work?

It seems like a long time before Father gets back.

"Did you find the bear?" Mother calls.

"I found him, all right!" Father says.

Arthur sighs. It looks as if his wish didn't come true after all. . . .

"We have a guest!" Father beams. "Look—Mr. Bear is here to share our Christmas!"

"Hi," mumbles the bear. "I don't want to put you all to any trouble."

"No trouble at all," Father laughs. "Make yourself comfortable. Have a few cookies!"

"I would love some cookies," the bear says softly.

As Father bustles around making Mr. Bear welcome, Mother can only stare. "What happened?" she whispers into Arthur's ear. "I never thought your father would do such a thing!"

Arthur smiles a secret smile. "See? The button is magic! It made my wish come true!"

At last they all sing Christmas carols together—Arthur, Mother, Father, and Mr. Bear.

It really is a very merry Christmas.